P9-CRE-670

DOG TO THE RESCUE

SEVENTEEN TRUE TALES OF DOG HEROISM

Jeannette Sanderson

AN
APPLE
PAPERBACK

SCHOLASTIC INC.
New York Toronto London Auckland Sydney

Photo Credits

Chips, Nemo: U.S. Air Force, Military Working Dog Squadron; **Dutchess, Grizzly Bear, Hero, Leo, Mijo, Mimi, Patches, and Zorro:** The Quaker Oats Compay; **Eve:** The Humane Society of Indianapolis; **Sabre:** Gordon Patenaude; **Spuds:** *The Herald*, Rock Hill, South Carolina; **Tina:** Nora Ann Martyniak.

If you purchased this book without a cover, you should be aware that this book is stolen property. It was reported as "unsold and destroyed" to the publisher, and neither the author nor the publisher has received any payment for this "stripped book."

No part of this publication may be reproduced in whole or in part, or stored in a retrieval system, or transmitted in any form or by any means, electronic, mechanical, photocopying, recording, or otherwise, without written permission of the publisher. For information regarding permission, write to Scholastic Inc., 730 Broadway, New York, NY 10003.

ISBN 0-590-47112-0

Copyright © 1993 by Jeanette Sanderson.
All rights reserved. Published by Scholastic Inc.
APPLE PAPERBACKS is a registered trademark of Scholastic Inc.

12 11 10 9 8 7 6 5 4 3 2 1   3 4 5 6 7 8/9

Printed in the U.S.A.   40

First Scholastic printing, October 1993

Acknowledgments

I would like to thank the many people who helped me write this book.

Scores of people from across the country assisted me in collecting and researching these stories. Many of these people were librarians. My thanks to American Kennel Club librarians; Danbury, CT, librarians; Hugh Howard at the Pentagon Library; Nancy Howland at the White Plains, NY, Library; Tom Leonard at the Cape May, NJ, Library; and Ellen Strong at the Library of William and Mary College.

Newspapers were also a valuable resource in my research. My thanks to Rhonda Coleman of the *Vallejo Times-Hearald*; Jeanine Hinchliff of the *Priest River Times*; and the editorial librarians at the editorial librarians at *The Sacramento Bee*.

People from a variety of other organizations also provided me with a good deal of background information. I would especially like to thank the people at the Quaker Oats Company; Melissa Bennett of the Massachusetts Society for the Prevention of Cruelty of Animals; Hildegarde Brown of the Military Working Dog Training Center at Lackland Air Force Base in Lackland, TX; Kay Clark of the American Humane Association; Kevin Conroy of the United States Police Canine Association, Inc.; Jeannie Keating of the Humane Society of Indianapolis; Chris Martin of the Texas Veterinary Medical Association; and Betty Peck of the Excelsior Lake Minnetonka Historical Society in Excelsior, MN.

To the proud dog owners I spoke with — Linda Krause, Nora Martyniak, Gordon Patenaude, Gay Tanis, and Kathie Vaughn — thank you for sharing your stories with me.

I would also like to thank my husband, Glenn, for his patience in listening to many, many dog stories and my daughter, Catie, for her many smiles. Thanks, too, to Patsy, Alice, and Mrs. O. for their support.

Finally, my thanks to brave dogs everywhere — and to these seventeen dogs in particular — for giving us stories to tell.

Dedicated to the memory of Tom DeLuca

Contents

Caesar   1
Chips   7
Dutchess   13
Eve   17
Grizzly Bear   22
Hero   27
Leo   32
Mijo   36
Mimi   40
Nemo   44
Pashka   50
Patches   56
Sabre   62
Spuds   68
Tina   71
Villa   77
Zorro   84

Caesar

The Glazer brothers trained their pet German shepherd to do many things. Like most dogs, Caesar could sit, shake hands, and fetch. Caesar also had a special trick. He could deliver. The brothers would buy something at the store and tell Caesar, "Take it to Mom." The dog would grab the package in his teeth and carry it straight home to Mrs. Glazer. Caesar's training would serve him — and the United States — well during World War II.

Irving, Morris, and Max Glazer wanted a German shepherd puppy. They had saved sixty dollars to buy it. The Bronx, New York, brothers went out looking for their new pet every Sunday. They drove all over in search of just the right dog. After three months, they found the black-and-gray pup at a Long Island kennel. His name was Caesar von Steuben. He was only nine weeks old, but already he looked like a conquerer.

The brothers were proud of their purchase. "He

just stood out as the best of the litter," Irving explained to his mother and father. The boys knew they made the right choice as Caesar grew into a big, beautiful, intelligent dog.

Irving, a teenager, was the youngest of the brothers. He spent the most time with Caesar. Irving often brought the dog to the park to play ball or go swimming.

The teen taught Caesar many tricks. He taught him to sit up, shake hands, and fetch. He taught him to stay. Irving would take Caesar somewhere and tell him to sit. He would then leave the dog for 15 minutes or more. When he returned, Caesar hadn't moved. "No one could budge him until I said okay," Irving said. "And if he was running and I told him to stop, he'd halt right in his tracks."

One of Caesar's best tricks was his ability to deliver. Every day, Mrs. Glazer would send one of her sons to the grocery store or the bakery with Caesar. The boy would buy what she wanted, then give it to Caesar. "Take it to Mom," he would command. Caesar would take the package in his teeth and head straight home without stopping. This "trick" let the brothers stay out a while longer.

The beginning of World War II nearly brought an end to Caesar's days as a messenger. Morris, Max, and Irving all entered the service. Mr. and Mrs. Glazer found it difficult to take care of Caesar without their sons' help. They thought of selling him. But they hated to do that. Then one day they heard that the Army was looking for dogs to help in the war effort.

The Glazers gave Caesar to Dogs for Defense. This was an organization of American civilians who trained dogs for the war effort. Caesar's talents could be put to good use in the war.

The Army gave Caesar basic training and advanced schooling as a messenger. On October 4, 1943, Caesar shipped out with the first Marine dog platoon. They sailed for Bougainville, an island in the South Pacific. There the dogs and their handlers would join the fight against the Japanese. Caesar's two handlers were Private Rufus Mayo and Private John Kleeman.

The platoon reached the island on November 1. The American soldiers were greeted with heavy gunfire. They quickly ran to the dense jungle for cover. There they set up a command post.

Mayo led a company through enemy-ridden jungle to form a roadblock against the enemy. Caesar was part of that company.

Mayo was unable to communicate with the command post. Walkie-talkie radios failed to carry messages through the dense jungle. A telephone line had not yet been laid. Caesar was put to work as a messenger right away. He became the only means of communication between the front lines and the command post.

Caesar made several runs that first day. Grenades exploded around him. Gunfire erupted — sometimes it was directed right at Caesar. But the brave dog continued to carry his lifesaving messages.

By the second day, the Marines had laid a telephone wire. The Japanese quickly cut it, and Caesar continued his runs. He carried messages, overlays, and papers that had been captured from the Japanese.

On the second night, Caesar proved that he was more than a messenger. He also proved his usefulness as a watchdog. He and Mayo were to act as a listening post. They were located in a foxhole several hundred yards forward of the company. Here they could detect and warn the rest of the company of a surprise night attack.

When Caesar became very restless that night, Mayo went on the alert. The next thing he heard was the sound of a pin being pulled from a grenade — which means that soon it's going to explode. A second later he felt the grenade land at his feet. In the dark, Mayo reached for the grenade and flung it back in the direction he thought it came from. The next morning, eight enemy soldiers were found killed by the grenade meant for Mayo and Caesar.

Caesar continued his messenger runs the third day. The Japanese knew that the Marines needed Caesar to survive. They tried several times to kill the brave dog, but were always unsuccessful. By the end of the third day, Caesar had made his ninth successful run between the front lines and the command post. It was almost his last.

That night, Mayo and Caesar continued in their position as listening post. Shortly before dawn, the Japanese tried another sneak attack. Again, Mayo didn't hear the enemy soldiers, but Caesar did. Before the sleepy Marine could stop him, Caesar jumped out of the foxhole and ran toward the Japanese. Mayo quickly called Caesar back. As the obedient dog turned around, a Japanese soldier shot him twice.

A battle followed. During the confusion, Caesar disappeared. Mayo was worried sick. He contacted the command post to see if anyone had seen Caesar. No one had.

Mayo looked and found a trail of blood through the jungle. He followed it to the command post. There, lying in the bushes near Private Kleeman, was a barely conscious Caesar. The brave dog had returned to the safety of the command post and his other handler.

Mayo ran to the dog who had twice saved his life. He gently hugged him.

Meanwhile, several Marines made Caesar a special stretcher. They chopped two long and two short poles to make a frame. Then they fitted it with a blanket. One dozen Marines offered to carry the courageous canine's stretcher to the

5

first-aid station. Other Marines saluted as the wounded hero was carried by.

Mayo and Kleeman waited outside the hospital tent for word on Caesar's condition. They had to wait about 20 minutes. Then the surgeon came out. He said he had removed one bullet but he could not remove the other one. It had lodged too close to Caesar's heart. Would the dog pull through? The surgeon thought he might.

Caesar had to take it easy for a while. The Marines asked for daily bulletins on his condition. They snuck him food. Their attention and well wishes paid off. Caesar made a quick recovery and was back on active duty in about three weeks.

The Commandant of the Marine Corps, General Thomas Holcomb, wrote to the Glazers. He thanked them for donating Caesar to Dogs for Defense. He told them that their dog had saved the lives of many Marines.

Chips

When a dog bites someone, he usually ends up in the dog pound. At the very least, he ends up in a lot of trouble. In 1942, when Chips, a fighting dog from Pleasantville, New York, bit the garbage man, he ended up in the Army. That bite, and the dog who inflicted it, turned out to be a real lifesaver for American troops.

Chips joined the Wren household just before Christmas 1940. The husky/collie/German shepherd puppy became a guardian of six-year-old Gail and her three-year-old sister, Nancy. He played with and protected them at the beach, at the park, and around the neighborhood.

The dog was gentle with his mistresses, but he was tough with everyone else. Sometimes he was a little too tough. He bullied other dogs, cats, and even people. The Wrens' neighbors complained about Chips. The Wren family said their dog was just a little overprotective. Then Chips bit the garbage man. The Wrens had to admit that maybe Chips was too tough for the village of Pleasantville, New York. They donated Chips to Dogs for Defense. This organization of American civilians trained dogs for the war effort.

In the spring of 1942, Chips was enlisted in the Army's K-9 Corps. He was sent to Front Royal, Virginia, for basic training. Chips was taught to respond to such commands as No; Heel; Sit; Stay; Come; Crawl; and Up. After basic training, Chips received special training as a scout, guard, and messenger.

It was at Front Royal that Chips met his handler, Private John P. Rowell. Rowell trained with Chips for three weeks. Then the soldier and his dog were sent to Camp Pickett, Virginia. A few days later, Rowell's infantry company set sail for the invasion of North Africa. Chips was making history as one of four dogs in the first K-9 detachment to cross the Atlantic.

Enemy soldiers opened fire as Rowell and his company landed on the beach at Fedallah, French Morocco. At first, the sound of gunfire frightened Chips. But the dog quickly forgot his fear and learned what he had to do to survive. As planes dropped bombs overhead, Rowell quickly dug two shallow foxholes — one for him and one for Chips. When the planes passed, Rowell frantically began deepening his foxhole. Chips watched his handler and then, paws and sand flying, began deepening his own foxhole.

Two months of long marches followed. By day, the Americans pushed the enemy back. They rested at night. Chips and the other K-9s in the unit slept with their handlers in outposts to guard against sneak attacks. There were no casualties from sneak attacks in Chips's unit. The same could not be said for battalions without dogs.

In January, the Third Division, to which Rowell and Chips belonged, returned to the coast to rest. Chips's rest was cut short by a special assignment, however. United States President Franklin Roosevelt and British Prime Minister Winston Churchill were meeting for an historic conference in Casablanca. Chips and the other members of the K-9 Corps were needed to beef up security for this conference. Each night, Chips patrolled the area where the two leaders met and talked with their military advisors.

At the end of the conference, Roosevelt and Churchill took the time to meet Chips and their other four-footed protectors. Chips, like the other dogs, was too tired to appreciate the honor. At the end of this tour of duty, he ate a huge meal and slept for 12 straight hours.

Within months the outfit was training for the invasion of Sicily. In July, the American forces set sail for this island off the southern tip of Italy.

Rowell and Chips were part of the pre-dawn landing force. They had advanced about 400 yards up the dark beach when the sky was lit up by enemy machine-gun fire. It was coming from what looked like a grass hut up ahead.

Rowell remembers that, from then on, "things happened pretty fast." As American soldiers hit the sand, Chips jerked his leash from Rowell's hand. In a flash, he was inside the hut. Rowell recalls, "There was an awful lot of noise. Then I saw one fellow come out the door with Chips at his throat. I called him off before he could kill the man. Right afterward, the other fellow came out holding his hands above his head."

Chips suffered a powder wound and a scalp wound in the attack. The dog was quickly given first aid and returned to duty. Later that night he spotted a patrol of ten enemy soldiers. He alerted Rowell to their presence. Rowell took them as prisoners. Chips's prisoner count for the day was 12!

Word of Chips's heroism spread up the ranks. On November 9, 1943, Chips received two medals. He was awarded a Silver Star for bravery and a Purple Heart for wounds received in action. He was the first dog in United States history to receive these honors. Chips's medals were later withdrawn. Some people thought it wasn't right to award an animal an award meant for humans. But medals or not, Chips is a hero.

General Dwight D. Eisenhower later tried to congratulate Chips in person. But, again, Chips wasn't impressed by high-ranking officials. When Eisenhower reached out to pet Chips, Chips bit his hand! This hand belonged to the head of all American, British, and French forces in the Mediterranean war zone. Was Chips court-martialed for this act? Of course not! After all, he was just doing what he had been trained to do — be wary of strangers.

Chips continued to fight until the war in Europe ended. During his tour of duty, he saw battle in Italy, France, Germany, and Austria.

In the fall of 1945, Chips arrived back in the states. He was detrained at Front Royal, Virginia. And, on December 10, 1945, the canine war hero was discharged from the Army.

The Wrens had gotten wonderful reports of their dog during the more than three years he was away. "Your Chips is a dog to be proud of, and every member of the battalion that he is in is sure proud of him," one soldier had written them. The Wrens were proud of Chips. They were excited about his return.

After his discharge, Chips headed home to Pleasantville. He traveled by train, accompanied by six reporters and photographers. Mr. and Mrs. Wren met him at the station. Gail and Nancy hurried home from school to see him.

Chips didn't seem too much the worse for wear.

His once bushy tail was now a little scraggly. But invisible battle scars began to take their toll. What bullets couldn't kill, battle fatigue and kidney trouble could. Chips died just five months after his discharge, in April 1946.

Dutchess

Donald Phillippi and three of his children were enjoying their ride on Lake William in Mr. Phillippi's homemade boat. But the fun quickly ended when the boat overturned, throwing its occupants into deep water 150 yards from shore. Mr. Phillippi didn't know how he would get his children to safety. Only one of them could swim. Then he saw the family's dog, Dutchess, swimming toward them. Perhaps there was hope after all.

Johnny, eleven, Linda, ten, and Matthew, six, were excited as they piled into their father's homemade motorboat. Donald Phillippi was taking his children for an early evening ride on Lake William, which bordered their property. It was 6:30 P.M., and there was still some day left to enjoy.

Mr. Phillippi started the packed boat and headed out on the lake. The boat was small but fast. Mr. Phillippi gave it some gas. Then he and the children cruised around the lake and enjoyed the last of the beautiful September day.

Soon, however, it was time to go home. They were in the middle of Lake William when Mr. Phillippi tried to turn the boat around to head back to shore. But the boat didn't make the turn. It started filling with water and began to stand on end. Then the boat capsized and threw Mr. Phillippi and the children overboard into the deep water. They were 150 yards from shore, and neither Linda nor Matthew knew how to swim.

"We couldn't have been in a worse position," Mr. Phillippi said. "The boat was right down in the water and hard to hang on to. . . . The kids kept slipping off the boat. I had to hang on to all of them, but it was impossible. They were getting panicky and I was afraid they were going to start going under any second."

The frightened father didn't realize that help was on the way. The family's three-year-old German shepherd, Dutchess, had been lying on the shore in the family's backyard when the boat overturned. Mr. Phillippi didn't call to her — he didn't even know she was there — but the dog knew her master was in trouble. She plunged into the water and with powerful strokes swam toward the overturned boat.

When Mr. Phillippi looked up, he saw Dutch,

as she was affectionately known, swimming toward them. "I've never seen a dog swim so fast," he remembered. "She hardly seemed to touch the water, she was swimming at such a clip." Dutchess swam right up to Mr. Phillippi's side, "just as though she were offering help," he said.

Mr. Phillippi knew he had to act fast. He told Linda to grab Dutchess's collar. The panicked girl did as she was told. Dutchess didn't wait for a word of command. She immediately turned and began swimming for shore, towing ten-year-old Linda behind her.

Dutchess stumbled ashore after the long 150-yard swim. She deposited Linda safely on the bank. The exhausted girl collapsed. Then Dutchess turned to swim back to the boat and continue her rescue operation. But she saw that she didn't have to. A neighbor had witnessed the accident from his home on the other side of the lake. He was already there with his rowboat, pulling Mr. Phillippi and the two boys safely aboard.

"I'm convinced that if the other boat hadn't showed up, Dutch would have kept at it until she had all of us ashore," Mr. Phillippi said. "She was working just like clockwork. No human being could have done it any smarter."

Dutchess's bravery won her the affection of the children's mother, Ann Phillippi, who had never been too fond of the dog. The day after the acci-

15

dent, Mrs. Phillippi gave Dutchess her favorite treat — a nice long Sunday drive.

Dutchess's loyalty and bravery won her more than her family's admiration and affection. She was also named Ken-L Ration's 1958 Dog Hero of the Year.

Eve

The cab of the truck was filled with smoke. Kathie Vaughn pushed her dog, Eve, to safety. Then Vaughn, who is paralyzed from the waist down, frantically began to look for the pieces of her disassembled wheelchair. Eve kept jumping back up to the cab and grabbing at Vaughn. "No!" Vaughn told her. But the next thing Vaughn knew, Eve was dragging her out of the cab. Vaughn hit the ground hard and blacked out. She came to just in time to watch her truck explode.

Kathie Vaughn was ready to drive all night to an antiques show in Atlanta, Georgia. The Indianapolis, Indiana, woman had a brand-new truck, a tank full of gas, a trailer filled with antiques, and her dog by her side.

The 41-year-old woman pulled onto Interstate 65 and settled in for her 12-hour drive. But she wasn't even 20 minutes from home when she heard

17

a loud pop. Her truck swerved and started to go out of control. Vaughn quickly pulled over to the side of the road.

By the time she got there, smoke was filling the cab. It was coming from the truck's engine compartment, which was inside the cab. Vaughn took a quick look about her. She grabbed the can of Pepsi she had been drinking and poured it around the edge of the engine compartment. Nothing happened. The smoke kept billowing out.

Vaughn knew the smoke would harm Eve, her 104-pound rottweiler, before it would harm her. The dog's smaller lungs would fill more quickly than her own. So the woman reached over and opened the passenger-side door. Then she pushed Eve out of the truck.

By now, the cab was filled with black smoke. Vaughn new she had to get out quickly, too. But her multiple sclerosis had left her paralyzed from the waist down. She needed her wheelchair to get out of the truck — the drop from the cab to the ground was too great to jump.

Vaughn began looking for the pieces of her disassembled wheelchair. It was difficult to see anything through the thick black smoke. She found some of the parts, but not all of them. She was still looking as Eve jumped back up to the cab and grabbed her arm. "No!" Vaughn said, pushing the dog away. Eve jumped up again, and again Vaughn pushed her away.

At this point, flames began shooting out of the engine compartment. Eve jumped up again. The flames scorched her paws. The dog didn't care. She grabbed her mistress again. But this time Eve grabbed her mistress by the leg, where she couldn't feel anything. Before Vaughn knew what was happening to her, before she could say "No," Eve was dragging her out of the truck.

Vaughn hit the ground with a thud and blacked out. She came to a few moments later. She watched as the truck, which was about 10 feet away, exploded in front of her. Eve, still worried for her mistress, dragged Vaughn about 20 feet further away.

Minutes later, a state police officer arrived at the scene. He came running to see if anyone was hurt. The officer's quick movements frightened Eve. The dog lunged for the officer. Vaughn had to grab Eve by her collar and hold her back. Still, the dog wouldn't let the police officer any closer to her mistress than about four feet.

"Are you okay?" the officer called to Vaughn.

"I think so," she said.

"Can you walk?" he asked.

Vaughn explained that she was a paraplegic.

"Can you get to my patrol car?"

"I'll try."

The patrol car was about 25 feet away. Vaughn, still clutching Eve's collar, began dragging herself toward the vehicle. It was hard work. Her ribs had been bruised in the fall and she was in pain. When Eve realized what her mistress was trying to do, she helped pull her along until they both reached the patrol car.

From there, Vaughn watched the fire department arrive and struggle to contain the 20-foot flames that were now shooting from the truck. It wasn't easy. They had to cut into both sides of the vehicle before they could put the fire out. By then, the blaze had burned $250 in cash and thousands of dollars worth of antiques.

Despite that loss, Vaughn feels very lucky — and thankful — to have escaped with her life.

"I wouldn't be alive if it weren't for Eve," she said. "They say animals have no reasoning powers. But I say Eve had reason to go back into the fire. I had pushed her out of the truck and she returned, against all her natural instincts, to save me. And I'm here today."

Vaughn says that the family pet is "more clingy and protective of me than ever before. We took her to the junkyard where the truck is. As soon as she got close enough to smell the scent of fire, she wanted to leave. She tried to pull me away. The smell of it really worried her."

In 1992, the American Humane Association

awarded Eve its William O. Stillman Award for her bravery. An organization spokesperson said normally it takes at least 90 days to process an award nomination. But there was no debate about Eve's nomination. He said her award was approved in about two weeks.

Grizzly Bear

Polar Blu Samaritan von Barri was a long name for a big, gentle St. Bernard puppy. So the Gratias family nicknamed their dog "Grizzly Bear." That seemed like a good nickname for a St. Bernard who lived in Alaska. The Gratias family didn't know just how good a nickname it would turn out to be.

It was a cold spring day in Denali, Alaska. Mrs. Gratias was making lunch in the kitchen of the family's cabin. Mr. Gratias was doing chores somewhere out of earshot. Their two-year-old daughter, Theresa, was sleeping in the room just inside the front door. Grizzly Bear was in the kitchen with Mrs. Gratias. The 20-month-old St. Bernard was lounging lazily by the kitchen table.

Mrs. Gratias stopped chopping onions for a minute. She thought she heard a noise outside the cabin. Grizzly opened his sleepy eyes and lifted his heavy head. "Oh, it's probably just the wind,"

Mrs. Gratias said. She went back to making lunch.

Grizzly didn't go back to lounging. The dog was alert now. Years of fine breeding had sharpened his senses. He knew the sounds of the house. He knew the sounds of his masters' comings and goings. He knew the sounds of the forest that surrounded the cabin. He knew the sounds of the wind. And he knew that the sounds he heard weren't any of those things.

By now, Mrs. Gratias also realized that she was hearing more than the wind. "I *do* hear a noise!" she said. "There's something in the yard." She put her knife down on the cutting board. "It's probably nothing more than some birds fighting over scraps. But I better take a look, just to be sure."

Grizzly Bear stared at his mistress as she wiped her hands. "Oh, all right," she said. "You might as well get some exercise, too." Mrs. Gratias untied the leash that had bound Grizzly Bear to the table.

Mrs. Gratias opened the front door, the only door in the house. Grizzly Bear ran out. Mrs. Gratias stopped to look at her daughter. Theresa was still sound asleep. Mrs. Gratias decided to leave the door to the cabin open, since she was just running out for a minute.

As Mrs. Gratias walked toward the backyard, the noises grew louder. She knew something was back there, but what? She hurried around the corner, then stopped dead in her tracks. A grizzly bear cub was rummaging near the back wall of the cabin. The hungry cub was looking for something to eat after months of hibernation.

"Oh my goodness!" Mrs. Gratias said. She knew she didn't have much to fear from the cub, which was just as startled by their meeting as she was. Mrs. Gratias had a much bigger concern — the cub's mother. Mrs. Gratias knew enough about wildlife to know that grizzly bear cubs are seldom far from their mothers. These mothers are very protective of them. If they become separated from their cubs, they can be the most dangerous creatures in the world.

Mrs. Gratias let out a terrified scream as she remembered that she had left the front door open. "Theresa!" she shouted. She ran back to the front of the house. She had to protect *her* baby.

As she rounded the corner Mrs. Gratias came face-to-face with her worst fear — the mother grizzly. The bear raised itself up to its full eight-foot height. It grabbed at Mrs. Gratias with its huge paws. But the woman only thought of one thing — getting to the front door to protect her daughter.

Mrs. Gratias quickly tried to sidestep the enraged animal. But she slipped on the icy ground. She lay there, stunned, as the grizzly dropped to all fours and came at her in all its fury.

The grizzly dragged its huge claws across Mrs. Gratias's cheek. Blood gushed out as the bear continued its attack and sank its paw deep into Mrs. Gratias's shoulder. Then the grizzly opened its huge mouth and bent down to inflict what might have been a final, deadly wound.

Mrs. Gratias struggled, but she was too badly wounded to be much of a match for her enemy. With the bear's open mouth about to close in on her, a flash of brown-and-white fur flew before her eyes. It was Grizzly Bear, *her* Grizzly Bear.

The 180-pound dog hurled himself at the real grizzly's chest. The bear fell back from the force of the attack. Then it roared with rage and came back at Mrs. Gratias. But the dog continued his attack. Grizzly slashed at the bear with his teeth and claws. He jumped and barked at the bear. He kept himself between the bear and his wounded mistress.

Mrs. Gratias watched in horror. Finally, the terror and the loss of blood proved too much for the woman. She lost consciousness.

When she came to, Grizzly, her Grizzly, was licking her face, trying to revive her. She was confused for a moment. Then she remembered what had happened. Was Theresa okay?

Mrs. Gratias struggled to her feet and ran to the open door. She held her breath as she looked inside. But everything was as it should be. There was Theresa, still fast asleep. Mrs. Gratias took a quick look around. The grizzly bears were gone. Her own Grizzly, bloody and dirty, lay down next to Theresa and wagged his tail. He had done his good deed for the day.

Mrs. Gratias recovered from her wounds. Grizzly wasn't even wounded — the blood on his fur must have been the bear's or his mistress's.

"You saved both our lives," Mrs. Gratias said. She rewarded Grizzly Bear with a huge hug. Ken-L Ration awarded Grizzly Bear a gold medal, and named him the 1970 Dog Hero of the Year.

Hero

The Jolleys of Priest River, Idaho, could have chosen any name for their beautiful new purebred collie. They chose Hero. As it turned out, they couldn't have chosen a better name.

Mrs. Jolley took real pride in Hero. The young merle collie was friendly and bouncy. And he was beautiful. Hero had long, thick blue-gray fur, a long, lovely face, and dainty feet. Mrs. Jolley entered him in dog shows. She was sure he'd be a champion some day.

It was easy to see that Hero preferred the Jolley farm to the show ring. Like his collie ancestors, Hero was happiest herding the farm animals. And he was a good herder. Mrs. Jolley felt like she didn't have a choice. She put her show-dog dreams for Hero on hold and let him drive the animals. That's what the dog was doing on the day he truly earned his name.

It was late afternoon in February, 1966. Mrs. Jolley left the house with Hero and her three-year-old son, Shawn. She sent Hero to round up the horses that were grazing in the distance. Then she and Shawn went into the big barn, leaving the door open for Hero to drive in the horses.

Mother and son climbed the narrow stairs that led up to the hayloft. Shawn played in the hay for a few minutes, running and sliding on the slippery stuff. Then he ran back down the stairs. Mrs. Jolley picked up a pitchfork and went to work. She pitched mounds of hay through a hole in the floor to the horses' stalls below. Mrs. Jolley was working so hard that she didn't realize Shawn was no longer nearby until she heard him scream.

The scream came from below. Mrs. Jolley looked through the hole in the floor and saw Shawn running across the barn floor. His screams were nearly drowned by those of the wild stallion that thundered after the boy.

Mrs. Jolley shouted for Hero. She hoped he would be near enough to hear her desperate plea. Then she dropped her pitchfork and rushed to the stairs.

"Run, Shawn, run!" Mrs. Jolley called. The boy's only hope was the tractor on the other side of the barn. If he reached it, he could slide under it. Then he would be out of harm's way.

Seconds seemed to last hours. The raging horse

was right on Shawn's heels as the boy ran across the barn. At last, Shawn reached the tractor. But what should have been Mrs. Jolley's relief quickly turned to horror. As Shawn tried to slide under the tractor, his denim jacket got caught on a metal bolt. He was trapped! He couldn't move in any direction. The young boy screamed in terror. The giant black horse raised its front feet to stamp out the boy's life.

At this horrible moment, a mass of blue-gray fur came flying through the air. It was Hero. The dog flew right into the stallion's face and clamped his strong jaws on the horse's nose. And he kept them there. Pain made the horse even wilder. He flung his head from side to side trying to shake off Hero. The horse finally succeeded in flinging Hero against the side of the tractor. The dog hit it hard and collapsed in a heap.

With the dog out of his way, the blood-stained horse reared up again. But pain couldn't stop Hero from protecting his young master. The dog was up and once again hurling himself at the horse. He positioned himself between Shawn and the wild stallion. He snapped and he clawed and he leapt at the horse that was fifteen times his size.

Hero kept this up even though he was taking quite a beating. More than once the stallion's iron-rimmed hooves caught Hero in the mouth. More than once they landed on his front paws.

The brave dog ignored his pain and fought on to keep the horse at bay. This bought Mrs. Jolley the time and space she needed to reach Shawn. Mrs. Jolley had to hurry. The two animals were locked in a vicious battle just feet from where she knelt. She quickly untangled Shawn's jacket and pushed him under the tractor.

With her son safe, Mrs. Jolley grabbed a stick to try to save the life of her Hero. She poked and jabbed the horse. But the wild animal continued to pounce on Hero. Then, all of a sudden, the horse lost interest in the fight. He turned and ran for the door. Hero ran after him. The dog kept up the chase until the horse was a safe distance away. Then he sank to the ground, with blood pouring from his nose and mouth.

Mrs. Jolley ran to Hero. She scooped him up and carried him to her car. Then she and Shawn drove 45 miles to the veterinarian's office.

Hero was near death. The dog had suffered severe internal injuries. Five of his ribs had been broken. Four of his teeth had been knocked out. And his front paws had been crushed.

Another dog might not have made it. But Hero had proven himself to be a fighter. In five short weeks he was almost fully recovered. And Mrs. Jolley had him back in the show ring. Hero must have looked pretty good. The judges awarded him three more points toward the title of "champion."

Of course, the Jolleys already knew Hero was a champion. After all, he had lived up to his name. The Ken-L Ration company thought Hero was a champion, too. They named the collie from Priest River, Idaho, America's Dog Hero of the Year for 1966.

Leo

The Callahan children were playing catch with their dogs near the creekbed. Eleven-year-old Sean Callahan knelt down to pick up more sticks to toss. Instead, he came face-to-face with a diamondback rattlesnake. Luckily for Sean, the family's standard poodle quickly responded to the frightened boy's cries for help.

It was a hot August afternoon in Hunt, Texas. Bud Callahan drove his two children, Sean and Erin, to cool off at Honey Creek, near the Guadalupe River. The family's two dogs, Leo and Boo, had also piled into the Jeep to join the outing.

As soon as Mr. Callahan stopped the car, the kids and dogs scrambled out onto the creekbed. Sean, eleven, and Erin, nine, immediately began looking for sticks to toss to the dogs. "Go get it boy!" Sean called as he tossed a stick to Leo, a white standard poodle. Erin picked up a stick and threw it to Boo, a big black Labrador retriever. "Fetch!" she called.

The game continued downstream. Sean ran ahead and Erin ran after him. The boy stopped to gather more sticks at the foot of a cypress tree. But when he knelt down to pick them up, he found more than he was looking for. There, among the roots of the tree, lay a diamondback rattlesnake.

The rattlesnake had obviously felt the vibrations of Sean's approach. And its forked tongue had picked up the boy's scent. Sean wouldn't get the benefit of the rattlesnake shaking its tail in warning. The five-and-a-half-foot viper was already coiled and ready to strike.

Sean screamed as the snake's head bobbed back and forth. The snake was preparing to strike at Sean and inject his head or chest with its deadly venom. But Leo had heard Sean's cry for help and had come running. The dog saw the snake rear its head as it was about to strike. The 50-pound dog quickly jumped between the snake and his master. The snake opened its mouth revealing two white fangs for just a moment before sinking them into Leo's skull.

The force of this bite sent Leo toppling backward. The snake slithered forward and struck Leo again.

The poison began to take effect immediately. Leo began to feel numb and sluggish. But he would not give in that easily. He heard the children's screams. He had to protect them. So the dazed dog leapt at the hissing creature in front of him. He missed, and the snake struck again. This bite was close to Leo's left eye.

Mr. Callahan heard his two children screaming. He rushed to the cyprus tree and found them frozen in fear. While Leo continued to take the snake's venom, Mr. Callahan got Sean and Erin to the safety of the Jeep. Then he returned to help Leo.

Mr. Callahan found the white dog covered with blood and unable to move. The snake had slithered off, his dirty work done. Mr. Callahan scooped Leo up and carried him to the Jeep. Then he quickly drove back to the family's ranch.

Mrs. Callahan frantically tried to reach a veterinarian. She finally contacted Dr. William Hoegemeyer in Kerrville, fourteen miles away.

By the time Dr. Hoegemeyer saw Leo, the snake's poison had been cruising through the dog's body for nearly an hour. The deadly stuff had swelled Leo's head and neck to incredible proportions. His face was unrecognizable. His collar was strangling him. Mrs. Callahan had to cut it off so it wouldn't choke him to death.

The doctor examined the critically injured dog. Leo's face was so swollen, Dr. Hoegemeyer couldn't see his left eyeball.

"There is so much trauma here," the doctor told

the Callahans. "And the damage to the tissue is so extensive. Well . . . I doubt he'll make it."

Dr. Hoegemeyer gave Leo anti-poison medication. He didn't think it would do much good. Dogs injured as seriously as Leo seldom survived. But the doctor wanted to do everything he could for the brave dog who saved Sean Callahan's life.

Leo fought for his life as hard as he had fought for Sean's. And this second fight was just as successful. Leo survived — without brain damage, and without losing sight in his battered left eye.

Dr. Hoegemeyer called Leo's recovery "remarkable." He said that the dog's size and weight worked in his favor. But a major factor in Leo's survival was his extraordinary will to live.

Leo's heroic rescue did not go unnoticed. Ken-L Ration named him 1984 Dog Hero of the Year. And in 1986, the Texas Veterinary Medical Association inducted Leo into the Texas Pet Hall of Fame.

Mijo

Philiciann and Mitchell Bennett liked to play by the water-filled gravel pit not far from their home. The sister and brother often brought their dog, Mijo, along with them. At 180 pounds, the St. Bernard was a powerhouse. The Bennetts knew Mijo was strong, but they didn't truly appreciate her strength until the day Philiciann fell into the gravel pit.

"Can we take Mijo for a walk?" Philiciann and Mitchell Bennett asked their parents after the family finished dinner. Their parents told them to go ahead. It was a beautiful September day. The fresh air would be good for them.

Philiciann called Mijo. The St. Bernard, with her white barrel chest, brown moustache, and brown eye patches, came running. She was always ready to go for a walk.

Eleven-year-old Mitchell waited while his

13-year-old sister hooked the leather leash on Mijo's sturdy chain collar. Then the three set off on their adventure.

They ran and played until they reached the edge of a water-filled gravel pit. This was one of their favorite places to visit. The children stared into what looked like a giant bowl.

"Look how high the water is," Mitchell said.

"I know," Philiciann said. "I haven't seen it this high for weeks. It must be because of that big rainstorm we had."

Mijo didn't want to stand around while the children talked. She tugged at her leash.

"Oh, okay," Philiciann said. She unhooked the leather leash from the chain collar. The dog ran around the two children.

Philiciann folded the leather leash and put it in her pocket. As she did so, she lost her footing. The ground, softened by rain, was sliding beneath her. Before she knew it, Philiciann was in ice cold water up to her neck.

Philiciann was a strong swimmer. Her first instinct was to "push off" the mud below her and swim to safety. But when she did this, she was horrified to realize that the mud was like quicksand. When she tried to push off, her feet sank even deeper! Now the water was up to her chin.

"Help!" she cried.

Mitchell was surprised to see his sister in the water. He wasn't sure how she got there.

"Help me!" Philiciann called again. "I can't move. My feet are stuck."

Mitchell began climbing down the steep embankment to reach his sister. He had to rescue her. He didn't know that the ground beneath his feet might betray him at any moment. He didn't know that his strength would be no match for the powerful grip of the mud beneath Philiciann's feet.

Luckily for Philiciann and Mitchell, Mijo had also heard Philiciann's cries. The St. Bernard bounded off the edge of the pit and into the icy water. She swam toward Philiciann. Then she seemed to circle aimlessly in front of her.

"Come, Mijo," Philiciann called. But the dog disappeared beneath the surface. Philiciann almost lost hope. Then the dog came up directly beneath her.

Philiciann desperately grabbed the chain collar around Mijo's neck. Then she held on for her life. Mijo took several powerful strokes. These yanked Philiciann free of the treacherous grip of the mud. Then the dog towed the terrified 105-pound girl to the safety of a nearby bank. Philiciann didn't dare let go of her rescuer's collar until she was certain they were on firm ground. Mitchell then scrambled to join them.

Ken-L Ration named Mijo its 1967 Dog Hero of

the Year for her bravery in rescuing Philiciann Bennett. Mijo might also have indirectly saved Mitchell's life. If the dog hadn't been there, the boy would have gone into the water to save his sister. Then they both might have drowned.

Mimi

What kind of courage can you expect from a miniature poodle who is afraid to climb stairs? In the case of Mimi, a lot. Mimi braved dense smoke and flames to rescue her owners from fire. She even braved the stairs.

"I am a heavy sleeper," Nicholas Emerito says. "I don't know what would have happened if it weren't for that dog."

Mr. Emerito is remembering the night of January 30, 1972. He had fallen asleep watching a late show in the living room. Shortly before five in the morning, the family's miniature poodle, Mimi, jumped on Mr. Emerito. She began barking, licking his face, and scratching his chest. Mr. Emerito finally awoke and looked around him in disbelief. The room was in flames. Smoke was filling the house.

For a moment, he panicked. His wife and five-year-old son, Peter, were asleep in the downstairs bedrooms. His other five children slept upstairs. How would he get to all of them in time?

Mr. Emerito soon realized he had a helper. While he rushed to wake his wife and Peter, Mimi ran to the stairs. This was a first. The tiny dog had never set "paw" on the stairs before. The only way she would go up or down the stairs was if she was carried. But now she knew there was no time for fear. Mimi bravely dashed up the smoke-filled and flame-engulfed stairway to wake the other children.

The apricot-colored dog raced into the girls' bedroom. She yelped and scratched and tugged at nightclothes until she woke Deborah, 15, Lisa, 12, and Patricia, 10. Then she ran into the boys' bedroom to alert Edward and Anthony.

Soon, with Mimi barking encouragement, Edward and the girls had made their way down the fiery staircase. But when they reached the front door, they realized Anthony wasn't with them.

Edward had to go back and get Anthony. Choking on the smoke, the 16-year-old fought his way back upstairs to get his brother. Mimi flew past him on the stairs. She was jumping on Anthony's bed and trying to wake the 14-year-old when Edward reached the room.

Anthony finally woke up and realized this wasn't a nightmare. It was real. But when he and

Edward reached the stairs, the real-life nightmare had gotten worse. The stairway was impassable. Their escape route was cut off.

Mimi, who was only 12 inches tall at the shoulders, made it down the stairs. But when she realized her charges hadn't followed, she turned around and ran right back upstairs to them.

Mr. Emerito realized his sons were trapped upstairs. He began shouting to Edward and Anthony. He put a ladder up to a second-story window and called for them to climb down it.

But the boys' rescue wasn't to be that simple. Before they could begin their descent, flames spilled out of the house, covering their escape route.

"Jump!" Mr. Emerito shouted. This was their only hope now. Anthony climbed out the bedroom window first. He took a deep breath and jumped. He safely landed in his father's arms. Now only Edward and Mimi were left inside the burning house. Mimi watched and waited for Edward to go ahead of her. There were a few anxious moments when Edward's foot slipped and one of his feet got stuck inside the window. But he managed to free it. Then he, too, jumped to his father. Then, when everyone else was out of the house, Mimi leapt to safety.

The fire was fast and furious. In no time it completely gutted the family's two-story house. The Emeritos escaped with just the clothes on their backs. But they were alive, thanks to Mimi. "If it wasn't for that dog, the whole family might have died," said Danbury, Connecticut, Fire Chief Joseph Bertalovitz.

Mr. Emerito was extremely grateful. He had paid just $50 for Mimi four months earlier. But, after the fire, he said, "I wouldn't take a million dollars for her." He also promised to feed her steaks for the rest of her life.

Mimi's heroic act earned her more than fancy dinners. It also earned her Ken-L Ration's 1972 Dog of the Year Award.

Nemo

He was the first hero of his kind to return from the Vietnam War. The welcoming committee watched him walk down the ramp of the plane that had just landed at Kelly Air Force Base. He was wounded — his right eye was missing and a scar ran from below his right eye socket to his mouth. But his wounds weren't what made him different. This hero was different from other returning Vietnam veterans because he was a dog.

Vietnam's sentry dogs were brave and fearless. Their efforts to help root out the Vietcong earned them the name "guided muzzles." Of the many dogs that served their country in this war, Nemo is probably the most famous.

The Air Force bought Nemo from an Air Force sergeant in the summer of 1964. The two-year-old black-and-tan German shepherd received sentry-dog training at Lackland Air Force Base in Texas. His serial number, A53A, was tattooed in his left ear and, in January 1966, he was sent to Vietnam.

Nemo and his partner became one of several sentry-dog teams belonging to the 377th Air Police Squadron at Tan Son Nhut Air Base near Saigon. These teams made up the base's first line of defense against the Vietcong. Each man and his dog spent the night alone patrolling an assigned area at the perimeter of the base.

The sentry-dog team's job was to spot and get rid of any Vietcong intruders. The enemy wanted to destroy the strategic base's aircraft and facilities. The sentry-dog teams were to see that that didn't happen.

With their keen senses, the dogs were usually the first to detect trouble. When something wasn't right, a sentry dog would make his master aware of it. He could do this with a look or with a movement. The security policeman would then notify the Central Security Control (CSC) of the possibility of trouble. Then the team would move in to investigate, with the dog in the lead. If it turned out to be the enemy, the handler would inform the CSC. Then the CSC immediately sent backup to assist the man and his dog.

In July, Nemo's original handler returned to the States. The dog was then paired with 22-year-old Airman Second Class Robert Thorneburg.

The two worked well together. This was important because their lives depended on each other. And the lives of everyone on the base depended on them. This became painfully obvious on December 3, 1966.

In an early pre-dawn attack, two Vietcong units tried to infiltrate the base. The sentry-dog teams got out word of the invasion. The 377th called out its troops and fought back. The enemy's numbers were greater, but the 377th fought hard. It was a long, grueling battle. Finally, after seven long hours, the base was once again securely in American hands. But the victory came at a cost. Three airmen and their dogs had died in the fighting.

The next day, Thorneburg reported for duty about three hours early. That was usual procedure. Handlers spent that time visiting their dogs, checking for any scratches, bites, or sores, and generally looking after their partners.

The sentry-dog teams that climbed into the back of the army truck that night were quieter than usual. Many of the soldiers were thinking about the events of the previous night. They were saddened by the loss of their fellow soldiers. They were also anxious about what awaited them on their patrols. There was a good chance that stragglers from the previous night's invasion could still be out there.

Thorneburg and Nemo pulled duty near an old Vietnamese graveyard about a quarter-mile from the air base's runways. They got out and began patrolling, side by side. They walked around the

46

old grave markers and looked out at the elephant grass that grew taller than a man's head.

It was a clear, starlit night. Nemo paused by a shadowy Vietnamese shrine. Thorneburg studied his dog. Nemo's eyes were glistening. His ears had perked up. The fur around his neck was standing on end. Thorneburg could tell that Nemo sensed something was out there. But before the handler could radio the CSC, that "something" opened fire. A bullet struck Thorneburg in the shoulder. Nemo was shot in the muzzle. The bullet entered under his right eye and exited through his mouth.

That might have been the sad end of the story. But Nemo refused to give in without a fight. Ignoring his serious head wound, the 85-pound dog threw himself at the four Vietcong guerrillas who had opened fire. Nemo's ferocious attack bought Thorneburg the time he needed to call in backup forces. These troops came in and took care of the guerrillas. Then they rushed Thorneburg and Nemo back to the center of the base for emergency medical care.

The base veterinarian performed skin grafts on Nemo's torn-up face. He did a tracheotomy to help the dog breathe. And he had to remove the dog's right eye, which was hanging uselessly out of its socket.

Thorneburg had to be evacuated to the United States Air Force Hospital at Tachikawa Air Base in Japan to recuperate. The handler and the dog who saved his life said their final good-byes.

Nemo recuperated at Tan Son Nhut. He received many get-well cards from American children. "Dear Nemo," one read. "I love dogs. . . . I hope you get well."

After the veterinarian felt Nemo was well enough, the dog was put back on perimeter duty. But it turned out his wounds needed further treatment. The Air Force decided to send him home to Lackland, where he could receive the best possible medical care.

Nemo flew halfway around the world accompanied by returning airman Melvin W. Bryant. The plane touched down in Japan, Hawaii, and California. At each stop, the Air Force's veterinarians examined the brave dog for signs of discomfort, stress, and fatigue.

Finally, the C124 Globemaster touched down at Kelly Air Force Base, Texas, on July 22, 1967. Captain Robert M. Sullivan, officer in charge of the sentry-dog training program at Lackland, was head of Nemo's welcome-home committee.

"I have to keep from getting involved with individual dogs in this program," Sullivan said, "but I can't help feeling a little emotional about this dog. He shows how valuable a dog is to his handler in staying alive."

Nemo spent his retirement at the dog training area at Lackland. He was given a permanent kennel near the veterinary facility. A sign with his name, serial number, and details of his heroic exploit designated his freshly painted home.

Nemo died on March 15, 1973. Until then, his presence at Lackland reminded students just how important a dog is to his handler — and to the entire unit.

Pashka

The small plane slammed into the side of a steep hill. The pilot and his passenger were thrown from the aircraft and badly wounded. The pilot staggered away to find help. The passenger couldn't move. He lay helpless in the cold and freezing rain. His chances of survival looked slim. But his Afghan puppy had also been on the flight. And Pashka wouldn't let his master die.

It was Steve Bennett's twenty-second birthday. And his roommate, Leo Piggott, had a special present planned. Leo was going to fly Steve to a birthday lunch at Nut Tree Airport on Sunday.

It rained Wednesday, Thursday, Friday, and Saturday. Steve and Leo had hoped the weather would clear by Sunday, but it didn't. They decided to go ahead with their plans anyway. The two men and Steve's four-month-old Afghan pup, Pashka, headed for the airport.

The weather had cleared enough for them to make their short flight from Buchanan Airfield, near Concord, California, to Nut Tree with no trouble. But by the time they had finished lunch, the storm had gotten worse.

The single-engine white Piper Cherokee took off from Nut Tree Airport at 2:30 P.M. in heavy rain. The storm tossed the plane about. The fog cut their visibility to near zero. This would be dangerous anywhere, but they were flying through Bassford Canyon, an area of steeply rising hills.

The pilot and his passenger knew they were in trouble. Five minutes after takeoff, the plane slammed into a steep hillside. The wings and tail were ripped off the plane. Then the cockpit and engine crashed farther up the hillside. Bennett's and Piggott's seatbelts snapped, and the two men were thrown from the plane. Somehow, Pashka managed to stay put.

Bennett fractured his pelvis in the accident. He couldn't move. Piggott suffered a dislocated shoulder and severe cuts and bruises, but he could walk. In a daze, he dragged himself away from the crash site to try to find help.

The storms of the last four days had dumped four inches of rain on the area. Piggott stumbled up and down Bassford Canyon's steep hills. His feet often got stuck and sank in the mud. He was freezing. Then he remembered Bennett. He thought, If I'm this cold while moving, imagine how cold Bennett must be. Piggott moved on.

Bennett was indeed freezing. But that night he had a warm comforter — Pashka.

Pashka suffered just a minor cut on his snout in the crash. But he was so stunned by it that he disappeared after the plane hit the hillside. No one knows where he went. Maybe he followed Piggott. Maybe he looked for help. Or maybe he was trying to find Bennett. It doesn't really matter, because Pashka did return to Bennett after nightfall. The orange-and-black puppy — at four months old as big as most full-grown dogs — curled up next to his master. He gave him warmth. And he gave him hope.

"I prayed and I hoped, but I never gave up," Bennett remembered. "The dog was my warm and friendly comforter."

While Pashka kept Bennett warm and hopeful, Piggott was feeling more and more cold and less and less hope. He had been walking for hours, but he seemed to be getting nowhere.

Finally, 22 hours after the crash, Piggott stumbled up to the door of Charles and Mattie Lou Jeffries' house. At first, the pilot startled the elderly couple. He pounded on the door like a madman and looked such a wreck, they thought he must be an escapee from prison.

But as soon as they opened the door they

learned they were mistaken. Words tumbled out of the wounded man's mouth. He talked about a plane crash and another wounded person still in the hills. Then he collapsed from shock and exposure. Mrs. Jeffries quickly called the sheriff and an ambulance.

Piggott was rushed to the hospital. An air and land search for the downed plane and wounded passenger began.

Civil Air Patrol pilots came in with a plane from the Travis Aero Club. They flew dangerously low over the foggy hilltops hoping for a glimpse of the wreckage. But the fog that made their mission dangerous also made it impossible to see anything. A helicopter set out with a flight surgeon. But the chopper was also forced to turn back because, with the fog touching the hilltops, there was no safe flying zone.

Land rescue efforts were equally tricky. The recent rain had left the hills so muddy that everything was getting stuck. In some places, the Jeep that carried one of the search parties sunk in 12 inches of mud.

Finally, at 3:20 P.M., a three-man team found the downed plane 1,400 feet above the valley floor. The wreckage was scattered over a 50-yard area. Bennett and Pashka were curled up around the base of a tree about 25 yards from where the plane had made impact.

Pashka didn't bark or whimper when the rescue

team approached. And he didn't budge from his master's side.

The searchers, who were on foot, used their walkie-talkies to call for assistance. They covered Bennett with blankets. Then they used parts of the wreckage to build a temporary shelter until help arrived. They built a fire nearby to keep Bennett warm.

Bennett told the search party that they had arrived just in time. "I knew that if I wasn't found by nightfall, I would have had it. I prayed all night that someone would find me and Pashka."

While the first rescue team tried to make Bennett as comfortable as possible, the backup struggled up and down slimy hillsides. They traveled as far as they could by Jeep. Then they carried the rescue basket on foot. Their progress was slow, but they finally reached the crash site. There they covered Bennett with more blankets and gave him warm coffee to drink.

Pashka still didn't budge from Bennett's side. When the rescuers gently lifted Bennett and placed him in the wire rescue basket, Pashka tried to climb in after him. The rescuers had to shoo him out. But Pashka was determined not to let Bennett out of his sight. He stayed within a few feet of his master during the long and difficult descent. Whenever the men stopped to switch carriers, Pashka would lick Bennett's face or nuzzle against his overgrown beard. He even tried to climb into the stretcher with his master a few more times.

The rescuers said over and over, "That dog is worth his weight in gold."

The two-mile trip down the muddy hill was rough. It took more than an hour to reach the Jeffries' house. Bennett and Pashka were finally separated at 6:20 P.M., when Bennett was taken to the hospital.

The doctors agreed with the rescuers' opinion of Pashka. They said that if it hadn't been for that faithful animal, Bennett's chances for survival would have been "mighty slim." That's because Pashka did more than keep Bennett warm. He also gave him reason to stay alive.

The American Humane Association awarded Pashka its William O. Stillman bronze medal for heroism. It was engraved PASHKA — FOR DEVOTION TO HIS MASTER, 1966. Steve Bennett said of the award, "This is one of the highest honors that I can think of. . . . I owe my life to my dog and I'm grateful that the American Humane Association has as much regard for Pashka as I do."

Patches

Patches was part collie and part Alaskan malamute. His collie ancestors were herders. They were smart and loyal. His Alaskan malamute ancestors were sled dogs. They were strong and able to endure harsh weather. Patches had all these traits. And he put them to good use the cold December night his master fell into the icy waters of Lake Spanaway.

Marvin Scott was exhausted. He had worked late at his furniture store. Now all he wanted was to be home relaxing in his warm house.

It was nearly ten o'clock by the time Mr. Scott pulled into his driveway. As he stepped out of his car, the wind slapped him in the face. The thermometer hovered around zero. It was a bitter-cold night, especially on the shores of Washington's Lake Spanaway, where Mr. Scott and his wife lived.

CHIPS

DUTCHESS

EVE

**GRIZZLY
BEAR**

HERO

LEO

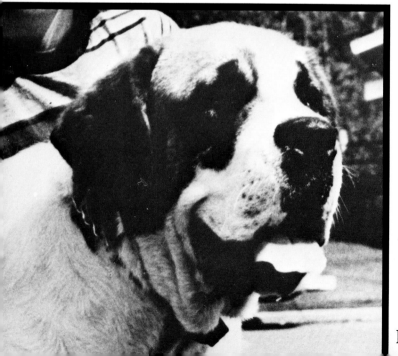

MIJO

MIMI

NEMO

PATCHES

SABRE

**SPUDS
WITH
DIRK
TANIS**

TINA

ZORRO

Mr. Scott bent his head and hurried up the walk. His ears were filled with the howling of the wind. But then he heard something else. It was a banging sound. And it was coming from down by the dock. Mr. Scott thought he knew what it was. He sighed and opened the door to the house.

When Mrs. Scott met her husband at the door, she could see he wasn't happy.

"Is something the matter?" she asked.

"I'm afraid we've got ice on the lake," he said. "With this wind, if it gets too thick it will punch a hole right through the patrol boat."

Mr. Scott knew he had to do something about that ice. He went to the closet to get his heaviest coat.

"Can't it wait until morning?" Mrs. Scott asked.

"I don't think so."

The tired man was about to head back out when his dog, Patches, came running to the door. He wanted to tag along. Mr. Scott was glad for the company in the raw night.

Patches trotted beside his master down the icy 300-foot slope that led to the dock. His master braced himself against the cold, but Patches didn't seem to mind it at all. The black-and-white dog was part collie and part Alaskan malamute. His ancestors had been Alaskan sled dogs.

When Mr. Scott reached the dock, he saw that a film of ice had formed around the boat. It was too dark for him to notice that the spray from the lake had frozen on the dock. There was a thin sheet of ice under his feet.

Mr. Scott picked up a piece of wood and began pushing at the boat's stern line. The ice was thicker than he realized. He pushed harder. As he did so, his feet gave way from under him. He tumbled forward and slipped off the icy pier. With a powerful thud he hit a floating dock and tore almost all of the muscles and tendons in both of his legs. Then the momentum of the fall carried him into the icy 15-foot-deep water. With his legs utterly useless to keep him afloat, and his heavy coat weighing him down, Mr. Scott began to sink.

The seriously injured man was sinking deeper and deeper, with no hope for survival. Then, suddenly, he felt his head jerk. Something had grabbed him by the hair. It was Patches. The dog had watched his master disappear into the icy, black waters, and quickly dove in after him.

Patches weighed 85 pounds. Mr. Scott weighed close to 200 pounds. But the dog, clenching a clump of his master's hair, paddled up with all his might. Finally, Patches and his injured master broke the surface. Now the dog had to pull the dazed, shivering man to the dock, which was 20 feet away.

The wind whipped the water around them. It forced water into Patches' nose and mouth as the dog struggled to reach safety. Patches was cold and choking. But he was his master's only hope. So he pushed on until they reached the dock and Mr. Scott was able to grab onto the edge of it.

Now Patches was in trouble. The brave dog couldn't get out of the water alone. And he was so exhausted from his rescue efforts that he wouldn't be able to fight this rough water much longer. If he didn't get out soon, he would drown.

Mr. Scott was so badly injured that he was only half aware of what was happening. But he sensed Patches was in trouble. And, somehow, he managed to muster the strength to push his rescuer up onto the dock.

Then Mr. Scott tried to pull himself up onto the dock. He could only use his arms, as his legs were totally useless. He pulled and pulled, but his body had been through too much. His terrible injuries, the freezing cold, and the water that he had swallowed caused him to black out. He lost his grip on the dock, slid back into the water, and went under again.

Patches jumped right back in after him. The dog grabbed his master's hair again. Then he pulled Mr. Scott to the surface and towed him about four feet to the dock.

Mr. Scott grasped the icy wood and tried to recover enough of his senses to figure out what to do next. Patches swam in circles around him, fighting the wind and cold that were beginning to get the better of him. Again, Mr. Scott saw the dog was in trouble. With the last of his strength, he pushed Patches up onto the dock.

Then Mr. Scott began screaming for help. But it was no use. The cries could barely be heard over the noise of the choppy water. And then they were stolen by the wind.

A shivering Patches paced the dock and watched his master. He stopped to lick Mr. Scott's icy hands. He whined and whimpered. But no one was coming to help. And, since Mr. Scott couldn't help himself, it was all up to Patches.

The dog firmly planted his four feet on the dock boards. He grasped the collar of Mr. Scott's coat with his teeth. Then he pulled with all his might. When Mr. Scott realized what Patches was doing, he began to feel some hope. This feeling allowed him to tap every last ounce of energy he had in his body. He pulled as Patches tugged. With Mr. Scott's help, Patches was finally able to pull him up onto the dock.

Once there, Patches still held on to Mr. Scott's collar. He waited until the gasping man regained his breath. Then the dog and his master — both soaked and shivering — began the 300-foot climb up the hill. Mr. Scott crawled while Patches pulled.

The climb was like torture. Both Mr. Scott and Patches were freezing and exhausted almost to the point of collapse. Patches' muscles were cramping. And Mr. Scott's already agonizing pain became even more unbearable on the icy, rock-studded incline.

Finally, the two were within a stone's throw of the back door of their house. Mr. Scott picked up a stone and threw it at the door. Mrs. Scott appeared at the door moments later. When she saw who it was, she ran outside.

Mr. Scott was rushed to Tacoma General Hospital. He was near death for 25 critical days. Pneumonia was a constant threat. And the massive operations Mr. Scott needed to repair his seriously injured legs posed many dangers.

But Patches' rescue efforts were not in vain. Mr. Scott's recovery was slow, but he did recover. Six months after the accident he returned to work, walking with the aid of canes.

For his amazing rescue, Ken-L Ration named Patches Dog Hero of the Year for 1965.

Sabre

*When Sabre arrived on the scene, the grand-
mother and her two-year-old twin granddaughters
had been missing for 12 hours. More than 50 pub-
lic safety officers, 150 volunteers, and two helicopter search teams had been unable to find the
trio. Would the air-scent dog be able to do what
they had not?*

Grace O'Connor and her two-year-old twin
granddaughters headed out blueberry picking
about 10:30 A.M. They didn't have to go far. There
were blueberry bushes laden with fruit in the
woods right behind the girls' Holden, Massachusetts, house.

The trio picked berries and played for about an
hour. Then Mrs. O'Connor decided to head for
home. The 64-year-old grandmother scooped up
the two toddlers and headed in what she thought
was the right direction. She walked along the
beaten path for some time. But, instead of leading

to her son's backyard, the path led to a dead end of deep, swampy brush.

Mrs. O'Connor tried another path. Then another. But they all seemed to end the same way. She and the girls were surrounded by heavy brush. The path home seemed lost.

After searching for about two hours, Mrs. O'Connor stopped to rest. She remembered that lost people were supposed to stay in one place, so they could be found more easily.

She couldn't stay put for long, however. Alexandra and Cassandra were hungry. So, Mrs. O'Connor moved again, this time to a blueberry patch. There the twins could fill their empty bellies.

"Alexandra and Cassandra thought they were on a picnic," Mrs. O'Connor remembers. "They thought it was a party. I kept them entertained. I was singing and praying. They kept saying, 'More, more.' "

At the same time that the toddlers were enjoying their "picnic," a massive search was getting underway.

Martha O'Connor, the children's mother, had returned home from doing errands around 2:00 P.M. When she saw that the lunches she left hadn't been touched and that the children's beds hadn't been napped in, she knew something was wrong. She called her husband at work and then ran out to search the area around the house. When she couldn't find her mother-in-law and her children, she called the police.

"The first thing we did was put the state police dog to the track," said Holden police Sergeant Kenneth D. Cook. "When that turned up nothing, we set up a line of people, just walking the woods."

More than 50 police officers and fire fighters from Holden and neighboring communities were involved in the search. They were joined by more than 150 volunteers, friends, and family members.

Grace O'Connor had no idea hundreds of people were combing the woods looking for her and her grandchildren. All she knew was that the long summer day was fading. She couldn't imagine anyone looking for them after nightfall, so she figured she'd best prepare to spend the night in the woods.

Mrs. O'Connor moved the children to a tree and built a barrier out of brush around them. "I wanted to keep animals out and keep the babies in," she explained.

Then Mrs. O'Connor undressed down to her underwear. She wrapped her pants and shirt around the girls to keep them warm. Then she cradled them in her arms. There, after another meal of berries, they would eventually fall asleep.

"I didn't think for myself at all," the grandmother says. "I was just interested in my little girls."

While Mrs. O'Connor was preparing for her

long night, the searchers were doubling their rescue efforts. The foot searches had turned up nothing. State Police helicopters were called in. They flew over a five-mile radius trying to spot something in the area. They couldn't find a thing.

Daylight faded along with hopes of finding the missing persons before morning. All traditional search methods had been exhausted. Like Mrs. O'Connor, the searchers kept hitting dead ends.

A U.S. Coast Guard helicopter armed with an infrared heat-seeker was called to join the search. This second chopper would scan the woods for any evidence of body heat.

Meanwhile, the police chief from a nearby town thought of something that might help. The previous week he had seen an air-scent dog demonstration. Unlike tracking dogs that follow a trail, air-scent dogs find the human scent that is in the air. Rain, sun, wind, or even another scent, can throw a regular tracking dog off course. An air-scent dog doesn't have to worry about these things. As long as a person is out there, giving off a scent, the dog can try to find it. Because of this, air-scent dogs have a very high detection rate — 83 percent — compared to 25 to 30 percent for tracking dogs.

The police chief immediately placed a call to Jeff LaFrenier of the three-member Massachusetts Air-Scent Rescue Dog Team that had given the demonstration. LaFrenier and Gordon Patenaude met at member Drew Paton's house with their K-9s. Then they hurried to the search site.

They arrived around 10:00 P.M. The Coast Guard helicopter was still conducting its ten-mile search. The men and their dogs had to wait to go into the woods until the chopper was finished. While they waited, they studied maps of the wooded search area. They divided it among the three teams. The Coast Guard finished its fruitless two-hour search at about 11:15 P.M. The men and their dogs entered the woods at 11:20.

Officer Gordon Patenaude and his 23-month-old German shepherd, Sabre, drew the west zone. It was about one mile long and a half-mile deep into the woods.

"Find them," Patenaude commanded. Sabre took off, nose in the air. He swept back and forth, trying to uncover a human scent.

With Sabre off-leash and in the lead, the dog and his handler made several passes through their area. But by the third go-round, Patenaude and Sabre were getting frustrated. They had been in the woods more than three hours and hadn't turned up anything. Then, suddenly, Sabre "alerted." He pointed his muzzle straight up into the air, then he ran into the thick brush.

A moment later, Patenaude heard singing. It later turned out that Mrs. O'Connor thought

Sabre might be a wild animal. She had begun singing to frighten him off.

Patenaude usually had to wait for Sabre to lead him to the find. That night, he just followed the sound of Mrs. O'Connor's song.

Patenaude found the children asleep in their grandmother's arms. He quickly checked to make sure they were all okay. Then he radioed that he had found the missing subjects and that they appeared to be safe and sound. He gave his location. Other search personnel arrived to help take the trio out of the woods.

Mrs. O'Connor and her two granddaughters were taken to a nearby hospital to be examined. They had all suffered from numerous mosquito bites, but were otherwise unharmed from their ordeal.

The O'Connor family had heaps of praise for Officer Patenaude and his dog, Sabre. "All that hi-tech equipment and it was a man and his dog who made all the difference," wrote the girls' aunt from Virginia.

Patenaude rewarded Sabre with the usual — a tennis ball and lots of praise.

Both Patenaude and Sabre were rewarded for their excellent work. They won both the Plymouth County Sheriff's Department's Silas Award and the United States Police K-9 Award for all of New England.

Spuds

Most people expect to spot dalmations at fire-houses. But what happens when these mascots find themselves in a house that is on fire? When Spuds, a dalmation from Rock Hill, South Carolina, found himself in a burning house, he lived up to his breed's fire-fighting reputation. The dog quickly woke his 15-year-old master. Then he rescued the family's kitten.

Dirk Tanis spent all of Saturday morning and part of the afternoon working at the church car wash. By the time the 15-year-old got home, he was hungry and exhausted. Since his stomach made more noise than his weary bones, Dirk headed straight to the kitchen. He poured some cooking oil in a pan and turned on the burner. Then he went into the den to wait for the oil to get hot enough to fry some onion rings.

The house was quiet and empty on this hot August afternoon. Dirk sat down on the recliner and waited for the *pop-popping* of the boiling oil. He never heard it.

"I was so tired that I just dozed off," Dirk said. "I woke up because Spuds was biting my hand." That surprised Dirk, because the family's four-year-old dalmation had never bitten him before. In fact, Spuds usually didn't pay much attention to his young master.

Dirk's senses quickly told him why Spuds was biting him. The teen's nostrils were filled with smoke. He looked toward the kitchen. Smoke was pouring out of the room and flames jumped from the pan of cooking oil he had left on the stove.

"The flames were up to the ceiling," Dirk remembers. "And the fire just started burning more and more."

The kitchen cabinets, the ceiling, and the woodwork were starting to catch fire. And the microwave above the stove had started to melt.

Dirk dashed into the kitchen and turned off the burner. He called 911, then fled the house.

Spuds was still inside. The dog had seen the family's five-month-old kitten, Gizmo, go into the kitchen. The flames had captured the playful kitten's imagination. She didn't realize the danger and she was so low to the ground that the smoke hadn't bothered her yet. Spuds quickly lifted her by the scruff of her neck and carried her out of the house.

When the Newport Volunteer Fire Department

arrived a short time later, the fire had burned itself out. Dirk's turning off the burner apparently cut the fire off before it really had a chance to dig in its heels.

Fire Department Captain Ben Roach was very impressed with Spuds's actions.

"It's the first time I've seen this odd occurrence where the dalmation — the symbol of the fire service — took care of its owner," he said. What he meant was that the family pet had acted like a fire rescue professional. If Spuds hadn't woken Dirk, the toxic fumes from the melting microwave would have killed him.

In 1991 the American Humane Association awarded Spuds its William O. Stillman award for his bravery. Kay Clark, the organization's secretary, noted another unusual aspect of Spuds's quick rescue.

"Although we have given the award to pets who rescue their owners, we have never had an animal rescue another animal," she said.

Tina

*Nora Ann and Stephen Martyniak didn't want
another dog. Then someone asked Mrs. Martyniak to take Tina. Tina had been abandoned. If
she didn't find a home, she would be put to sleep.
Tina didn't look like much. She was very sick.
But Mrs. Martyniak felt there was something special about her. Her husband couldn't see it. He
didn't want the dog. Mrs. Martyniak talked him
into adopting Tina anyway. Less than two weeks
later, Tina saved his life.*

Nora Ann Martyniak was trying to work but
she couldn't concentrate. Somewhere outside
there was a dog that wouldn't stop barking. Mrs.
Martyniak knew dogs had been abandoned in the
area in the past. She was afraid this dog might
have been abandoned, too. She left her office to
look for the dog.

Mrs. Martyniak searched around the plaza-
where her office was located. The dog wasn't out-

side anywhere. She listened more closely to the barking. It was coming from inside the dry cleaners.

Mrs. Martyniak went inside to see what the commotion was about. The first thing the dry cleaner asked her was, "Do you want a dog?"

"Not me," Mrs. Martyniak replied. "Not me." She and her husband had recently lost their dog of 15 years. She wasn't ready to take in another dog. But, unable to help herself, she added, "Can I look at it?"

The dry cleaner showed her the six-month-old black-and-beige mixed breed. The dog was not well. Her owners had abandoned her and she had been picked up by the Brockton Pound. The dry cleaner had taken her out of there, hoping to find a home for the dog with one of her customers. If the dog didn't find a home, it would be put to sleep.

Mrs. Martyniak looked at the dog. She was sick and she wasn't very well-behaved. But, still, Mrs. Martyniak felt there was something special about her. She told the dry cleaner she would have to talk to her husband about it.

"No," her husband said when Mrs. Martyniak asked if he wanted to adopt the abandoned dog. "We're free now. What do we want another dog for?"

"I just have a feeling," Mrs. Martyniak said. "There's something special about her."

Mr. Martyniak still wasn't interested in adopting Tina. His wife was ready to cry. She wanted Tina that badly.

Finally, Mr. Martyniak gave in. "Okay," he said. "Let's adopt her."

Mr. Martyniak didn't see anything special about Tina. She wouldn't mind what anyone said, she bit, she was wild around strangers, and she was terrible to housebreak. And, as an added "bonus," she needed hundreds of dollars worth of medical care.

His wife agreed that Tina wasn't a dog you would love from scratch. But still, even though she couldn't explain it, she knew Tina was special.

Tina hadn't been at their home two weeks when she showed the Martyniaks just how special she was.

One afternoon, Mr. Martyniak went outside to shovel snow. Mrs. Martyniak was in the kitchen chatting with a friend. She was holding Tina by the collar to keep the dog from pestering her friend. Tina could never leave company alone.

Mr. Martyniak came in from shoveling, changed his clothes, and went out to the kitchen for the newspaper. Tina didn't even bother looking at him, she was so interested in Mrs. Martyniak's friend. Then Mr. Martyniak went out to the den to read his paper.

A short while later, Tina's ears stood straight up. Her hair stood on end. And, with every ounce of energy in her body, she pulled herself out of Mrs. Martyniak's grasp. Then she ran into the den. Mrs. Martyniak was surprised. She had never seen Tina leave a room with company in it. But she figured that maybe the dog just wanted to go play with her husband.

Tina was in the den barking up a storm. Mrs. Martyniak figured the dog and her husband were playing. But the dog's barks seemed to get more frantic. It was impossible to have a conversation. Mrs. Martyniak excused herself and went to tell her husband not to get Tina so worked up.

When she got to the den, Mrs. Martyniak saw her husband sleeping on the easy chair with Tina jumping on top of him. The dog seemed to be pushing at his mouth with her muzzle. Mrs. Martyniak had seen her husband sleep through almost anything on that chair. But she couldn't believe he could sleep with Tina's barking, jumping, and prodding.

Mrs. Martyniak went to pull Tina off of her husband. But when she got closer to Mr. Martyniak, she gasped. He was turning blue. She looked more closely and saw that her husband had stopped breathing.

After calling for help, Mrs. Martyniak ran back to her husband. Tina was more frantic than ever.

She barked and pulled at Mr. Martyniak's shirt. She put her muzzle to his mouth as if she were trying to breathe for him.

The paramedics arrived in time to revive Mr. Martyniak. Then they took him to the hospital. It turned out he had had a convulsion. Doctors weren't sure why. Nothing in Mr. Martyniak's medical history would lead them to expect that something like this would happen.

That's what made Tina's actions so important. "He was in perfect health," Mrs. Martyniak said. "There was no reason why you'd think he wasn't sleeping." If Tina hadn't gotten her attention, Mrs. Martyniak said she would have gone downstairs to do laundry. And she wouldn't have been back upstairs for two hours!

"If not for Tina, it would have been all over," Mrs. Martyniak said. She doesn't know how Tina knew her husband had stopped breathing. All Mr. Martyniak remembered was feeling dizzy and putting the paper down. Mrs. Martyniak and her friend didn't hear a sound. Tina must have heard or sensed something.

"It seems like a life for a life," Mrs. Martyniak said. "Her life was saved, and she gave a life back."

Her owners say Tina is still, "an all-around monster." But they wouldn't trade her for the world. They swear by shelter animals. "Look what you can get," Mrs. Martyniak said. "Tina's a real hero."

The Massachusetts Society for the Prevention of Cruelty to Animals agreed. The organization awarded Tina its 1992 Animal Hero Award for saving Mr. Martyniak's life.

Villa

For centuries, Newfoundlands played an important role along the Atlantic coast. Fishermen relied on the big strong dogs to haul in nets, tow rowboats to shore, and rescue drowning men. In 1983, a Newfoundland named Villa showed that she, too, had the right stuff. When she heard the cries of 11-year-old Andrea Anderson during a raging blizzard, she didn't let her, or her ancestors, down.

"No school today!" Andrea Anderson and her two sisters shouted excitedly. School was cancelled because of a big storm on the Cape May Peninsula where they lived. The girls looked forward to having the day off.

They ran to the window and watched the heavy snowfall. They laughed at the wind. Like a mad housekeeper, the wind swept parts of the ground bare, while piling snow into huge drifts in other areas. These drifts would be great for building forts or digging tunnels. The girls couldn't wait to go out and play.

Next door, Dick and Lynda Veit bundled up to take their three Newfoundland dogs for a walk. They struggled with the wind to open their front door. They finally made it outside. Then gusts of frigid air pushed them about on the beach in front of their house. The dogs didn't seem to mind the below-zero windchill factor. Their thick fur kept them warm. But the husband and wife weren't so well-insulated. They decided to turn around and go back into the house.

Once inside, two of the Newfoundlands curled up in front of the fire to take a nap. But Villa was still restless. Though 100 pounds and almost full grown, she was still a puppy. At a little over a year old, Villa still had a lot of energy to burn.

The dog paced in front of the kitchen door. She wanted to be let out into her run. This was an enclosed area for the dogs that the Anderson girls had helped the Veits build.

Figuring that the dog had her thick coat to keep her warm, Dick Veit opened the door. Villa trotted out.

She wasn't alone in wanting to get some fresh air. The Anderson girls were outside playing in the snow. They shrieked as they threw snowballs at each other. They dug tunnels in the deepening snowdrifts.

Villa's ears perked up when she heard the girls.

They were her friends. In addition to helping build the run, they fed and petted the dogs whenever the Veits went away. Villa wagged her tail when she heard Andrea's voice. Andrea was Villa's favorite. The girl always had a special pat or kind word for her.

The girls saw that the Veits had let one of the Newfoundlands out, but they weren't sure which one it was. The snow was too thick for them to see more than the dog's big black shape. They might have liked to come over and play with the dog, but they couldn't. Their mother had made them promise to stay close to the house.

The wind and the cold were getting to be too much for nine-year-old Heather and fourteen-year-old Diane. The two girls decided to call it quits and go inside. Andrea hated to give in to the cold. She said she would stay outside and play just a little longer.

After a few minutes, Andrea had to admit that her sisters had had the right idea. She was too cold to play any longer. She started to walk toward the door.

Suddenly, a gust of wind lifted the 65-pound girl off her feet. It pushed her tumbling backward over a five-foot embankment. It continued to force her back toward the bay. Andrea tried to stand, but the wind kept pushing her back. She finally came to a stop 40 feet from home and just yards from the bay. But her trouble wasn't over yet.

She had tumbled into a snowdrift and was buried chest-deep in snow.

Andrea tried to claw herself out of the snowdrift. But she couldn't. And the snow kept building up around her.

She yelled for help. But no one in her house could hear her. Her mother was in the kitchen making dinner. Her father was in the living room reading the newspaper. Heather was taking a hot bath. And Diane was in her room watching TV. The only sound they heard inside the Anderson house was the howling of the wind.

Andrea kept yelling, but her throat was getting raw. She tried again to climb out of the snowdrift. But her arms and legs were so cold they were about as useful to her as lead pipes. She cried icy tears and tried to yell some more.

Villa, still in her run, stopped and perked up her ears. Weren't those Andrea's cries she heard over the howling of the wind? Yes, she was sure it was her. And Andrea must be in trouble.

Villa had never jumped out of her pen before. She'd never had any reason to. But now she had to find her friend Andrea. With all her might she hurled her powerful body over the run's five-foot-high wall.

Now Villa stopped to listen again. She knew she would have to rely on her sense of hearing to find Andrea. The snow fell so thickly that she could barely make out her own snout. Villa cocked her ears. Andrea's cries were fainter, but the dog knew where they were coming from. She charged through the snow toward the dunes.

Andrea was surprised and relieved when she looked up and saw the big, black shaggy dog. Villa licked Andrea's frozen face, providing warmth and reassurance.

Then Villa plowed a circle through the deep snow around Andrea. She trotted around and around this circle, her huge paws packing down the snow. When it was hard enough, Villa stood still as a statue and stuck her head out toward Andrea. The girl threw her arms around Villa's thick neck. Then the powerful dog walked backward, slowly pulling Andrea out of the snow.

Once out of the snowdrift, Villa dragged Andrea to an open area of the beach. Andrea stumbled to her feet and began to follow Villa back to her house. But the wind blew the cold and exhausted girl down again. Again, Villa stuck her head toward Andrea. Andrea grabbed hold of Villa's scruff and clung to the dog for her life. Whenever the girl's icy hands lost their grip, Villa would turn around and stick out her head again until Andrea could grab hold of her neck.

It seemed to take forever for Villa and Andrea to travel the 40 feet back to Andrea's house. Villa had a lot of work to do. In addition to towing Andrea, she had to plow a path for herself and her charge through the snow.

Finally, after about 15 minutes, Villa pulled Andrea up onto the porch of the Anderson house. She scratched at the door. As soon as the dog heard Mrs. Anderson's footsteps, she knew Andrea would be all right. The dog left her and trotted 50 feet through the blinding snow to her own home.

When Mrs. Anderson opened the door, Andrea stood there sobbing and shaking from the cold. She caught her breath just long enough to tell her mom, "Villa just saved my life."

Meanwhile, the Veits thought Villa was still out back in her run. So they were surprised when they heard scratching at the front door. They opened it and found Villa panting and covered with snow. Her tongue was hanging from one side of her muzzle. She dragged herself inside and collapsed next to the other dogs by the fire. They wondered how she had gotten out of her pen.

Just then the phone rang. It was Mrs. Anderson.

"Do you know what Villa just did?" she asked. Then she told the story of how Villa saved Andrea's life. Who knows how long Andrea might have lasted in that snowdrift, with a below-zero windchill factor, if Villa hadn't rescued her? As it was, she was frostbitten and frightened, but otherwise unharmed from her half hour in the freezing cold.

The Veits hugged Villa. "What a good girl!" they told her. And they gave her steak for dinner that night.

Villa received other prizes for her bravery. Ken-L Ration named her their 1983 Dog Hero of the Year.

Zorro

Zorro watched helplessly as his master, 26-year-old Mark Cooper, tumbled down the steep ravine and into the river. There was nothing the dog could do to stop the fall. But the eight-year-old German shepherd/wolf was not going to stand by and watch his master drown. Nothing — not even a dangerous 85-foot incline — could keep him from trying to rescue the seriously injured Cooper.

Mark Cooper carefully made his way up the steep trail in the Sierra Nevada Mountains near Sacramento, California. Cooper's eight-year-old German shepherd/wolf, Zorro, followed right behind him. The man's other hiking companions, two friends, were still a ways down the trail.

Over the edge of the cliff and far below, Cooper could see the river that ran through the steep ravine. It was highlighted by the November sun.

He was looking forward to reaching the top of the trail. The view of the entire ravine would be magnificent.

But suddenly, as Cooper neared the top of the trail, he lost his balance. He grasped for something, anything, as his feet fell from under him. But it was useless, there was nothing for Cooper to grab onto. Before he could even shout, he was over the side of the cliff and tumbling down the 85-foot incline into the ravine.

Branches, boulders, and sharp rocks scraped, bruised, and cut Cooper during the endless fall. They fractured his pelvis and tore up his insides. Cooper was seriously injured and unconscious by the time he plunged, facedown, into the river. Within minutes, the helpless man was caught in a whirlpool.

Zorro was the only one who had seen Cooper fall. The dog leapt over the cliff and half-ran, half-slid, the 85 feet down the steep slippery slope.

He dove into the cold water and swam toward his master. He fought the grip of the whirlpool's swirling waters as they tried to suck him under. When Zorro finally reached Cooper, he closed his powerful jaws around the man's backpack. Then, with every last ounce of strength he had, the dog pulled at him until he freed both of them from the whirlpool's suction. Zorro then swam to shore and dragged Cooper onto dry land.

Cooper was conscious now but in terrible pain. Zorro alternately licked his suffering master's face and howled for help.

Cooper's friends heard the dog's cry. They looked down the ravine and saw Zorro and the wounded Cooper. The slope was too steep for them to try to rescue Cooper on their own. They yelled that they would go get help. Then they were gone.

When the sun fell, so did the temperature. Zorro gently climbed on top of his shivering master to keep him warm. Cooper dug his hands into Zorro's thick coat. Zorro didn't move the entire night.

A rescue team found Cooper shortly after dawn the next morning. An Air Force helicopter was called in and airlifted the injured man out of the ravine. The eight-man ground crew that had found Cooper crowded back into their Jeep. There was no room for Zorro. They encouraged the dog to follow them as they slowly drove away. But Zorro was too tired or too confused about the whereabouts of his master. He stayed with them only a short distance, then dropped off.

When Cooper heard that Zorro was left behind, he cried. "I owe my life to him," Cooper said. "All I want is to get my dog back safely."

Word about Zorro spread. Volunteers formed search teams. Several days after Cooper's accident, two volunteers from the Sierra Club found

Zorro. He was next to the spot in the river where he had rescued Cooper, guarding his master's backpacking equipment. The dog was fine, though he was very tired and very hungry. The rescuers returned Zorro to the Cooper home.

Mark Cooper spent a long time in the hospital recovering from his injuries. But he felt very lucky — and thankful — to be alive. "I wouldn't be alive today if it wasn't for Zorro," he said. "He's a good dog."

Two organizations apparently felt the same way. Ken-L Ration named the brave and loyal dog its 1976 Dog Hero of the Year. Feline and Canine Friends, Incorporated, gave Zorro a Paws for Love Award for Heroism.

Best-selling author
R.L. Stine gives you...

Goosebumps

If you love to be scared, these books are for you!

☐ BAB49446-5	**The Haunted Mask**	$2.95
☐ BAB49445-7	**The Ghost Next Door**	$2.95
☐ BAB46619-4	**Welcome to Camp Nightmare**	$2.95
☐ BAB46618-6	**The Girl Who Cried Monster**	$2.95
☐ BAB46617-8	**Night of the Living Dummy**	$2.95
☐ BAB45370-X	**Let's Get Invisible!**	$2.95
☐ BAB45369-6	**The Curse of the Mummy's Tomb**	$2.95
☐ BAB45368-8	**Say Cheese and Die!**	$2.95
☐ BAB45367-X	**Monster Blood**	$2.95
☐ BAB45366-1	**Stay Out of the Basement**	$2.95
☐ BAB45365-3	**Welcome to Dead House**	$2.95

Available wherever you buy books, or use this order form.

Scholastic Inc., P.O. Box 7502, 2931 East McCarty Street, Jefferson City, MO 65102

Please send me the books I have checked above. I am enclosing $_____ (please add $2.00 to cover shipping and handling). Send check or money order — no cash or C.O.D.s please.

Name _____ Birthdate _____

Address _____

City _____ State/Zip _____

Please allow four to six weeks for delivery. Offer good in the U.S. only. Sorry, mail orders are not available to residents of Canada. Prices subject to change.   GB393